Presented by the Town and Country

Garden Group of the

Woman's Club of Accomack County

August 2008

Ellis Island

Risa Brown

Bethany, Missouri

Photo Credits:
Cover © Bill Mannig, Library of Congress; Title Page © Bill Manning; Page 4 © Alice McKernon; Page 5 ©
Photodisc; Page 7 © Luc Nijs, NPS; Pages 9, 10, 11, 13, 15, 17, 19, 20, 21, 22 © Library of Congress

Cataloging-in-Publication Data

Brown, Risa W.
   Ellis Island / Risa Brown. — 1st ed.
   p. cm. — (National places)

   Includes bibliographical references and index.
   Summary: Describes the journey and arrival of immigrants at
Ellis Island, from seasickness, fear, disease, and separation, to the
Statue of Liberty.
   ISBN-13: 978-1-4242-1368-9 (lib. bdg. : alk. paper)
   ISBN-10: 1-4242-1368-1 (lib. bdg. : alk. paper)
   ISBN-13: 978-1-4242-1458-7 (pbk. : alk. paper)
   ISBN-10: 1-4242-1458-0 (pbk. : alk. paper)

   1. Ellis Island Immigration Station (N.Y. and N.J.)—History—
Juvenile literature. 2. Immigrants—United States—History—
Juvenile literature. 3. United States—Emigration and immigration—
History—Juvenile literature. 4. Immigrants—United States—History—
Juvenile literature. 5. Historic sites—United States—Juvenile literature.
[1. Ellis Island Immigration Station (N.Y. and N.J.)—History.
2. United States—Emigration and immigration—History. 3. Immigrants—History.]
I. Brown, Risa W. II. Title. III. Series.
   JV6484.B76 2007
   304.8'73—dc22

First edition
© 2007 Fitzgerald Books
802 N. 41st Street, P.O. Box 505
Bethany, MO 64424, U.S.A.
Printed in China
Library of Congress Control Number: 2006940871

Table of Contents

A New Life

People from all over the world have dreamed of a better life in America. From 1892 to 1954, **immigrants** came into America through Ellis Island.

Statue of Liberty

Named for Samuel Ellis, who once owned the island, a center was built in New York Harbor to register immigrants. They could see the Statue of Liberty and New York City from their ships. They cheered to be in America!

New York

Ellis Island & Statue of Liberty

Journey

   The trip was hard, taking many weeks. Immigrants were crowded into the bottom of a ship. It was dark, dirty, and smelled horrible. The ship's constant motion made many people **seasick**.

So Many Unknowns

At Ellis Island, immigrants learned that they could be sent back. They were afraid. They stood in long lines with their **baggage**, hearing many **languages** they did not know.

Doctors

Doctors examined them. If they had certain **diseases**, they were sent back.

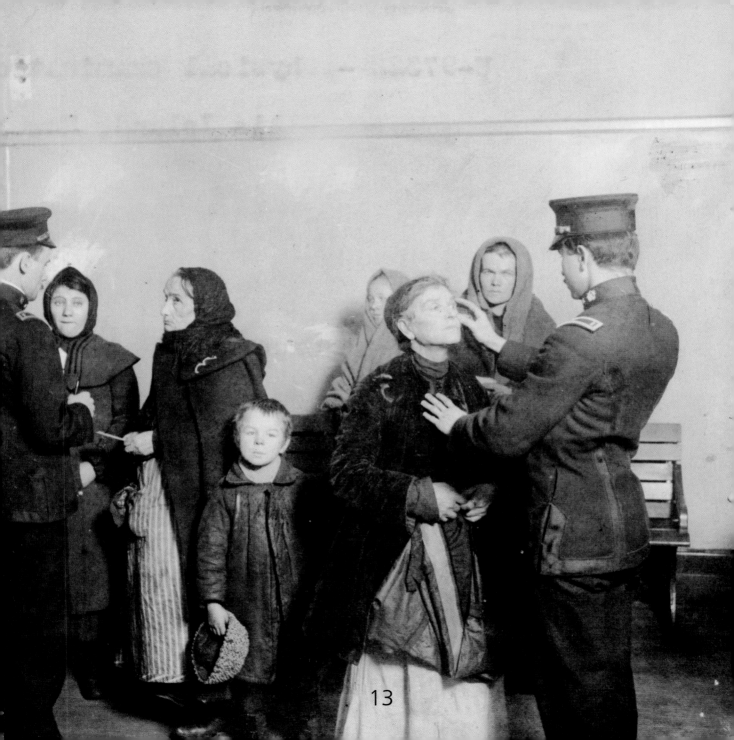

13

Questions

Then they were asked questions based on laws they did not know. If they gave the wrong answers, they could be sent back.

15

Separated

Sometimes mothers, fathers, and children had to go to different lines. They were scared, not understanding what was happening.

17

Reunited

Families were happy once they were together again! Relatives welcomed them to America. Sometimes people were even married at Ellis Island.

American Food

Many immigrants had their first American meal in the Ellis Island dining room. The food was very different from their food at home.

Moving Forward

When they left Ellis Island, immigrants began their new American lives.

Glossary

baggage (BAG ij) — sacks, baskets, or suitcases used to carry clothes and other personal items

disease (duh ZEEZ)— a sickness that could be passed on to someone else

immigrant (IM uh gruhnt) — a person who leaves one country to make a home in a new one

language (LANG gwij) — the words spoken and written in different countries

seasick (SEE sik) — a sickness brought on by the motion of ocean waves against a ship

Index

FURTHER READING

Anderson, Dale. *Arriving at Ellis Island.* World Almanac, 2002.

Knowlton, Marylee. *Arriving at Ellis Island.* Gareth Stevens, 2002.

Ruffin, Frances E. *Ellis Island.* Weekly Reader Early Learning Library, 2006.

WEBSITES TO VISIT

Because Internet links change so often, Fitzgerald Books has developed an online list of websites related to the subject of this book. This site is updated regularly. Please use this link to access the list: www.fitzgeraldbookslinks.com/np/ei

ABOUT THE AUTHOR

Risa Brown was a librarian for twenty years before becoming a full-time writer. Now living in Dallas, she grew up in Midland, Texas, President George W. Bush's hometown.